MR. ADVENTURE

Roger Hargreaves

Original concept by
Roger Hargreaves

Written and illustrated by
Adam Hargreaves

EGMONT

Mr Adventure liked going on holiday, but not the sort of holiday that you and I go on.

He thought beaches were boring.

He wanted the thrill and excitement of an adventure holiday.

He liked to go to places that would make your hair stand on end.

Mr Adventure went on holiday exploring remote frozen lands.

Epic expeditions across the white wilderness.

He went on holiday diving in the deepest oceans, discovering sunken wrecks.

He went on holiday trekking through far-flung, tropical jungles.

Sleeping under the stars with one eye open on the jungle creatures.

However, this year Mr Adventure had a problem.

He did not have enough money to go on one of his wild adventures.

To go on a new adventure he would need to get a job.

And so that's what he did.

He got a job as a postman.

But being Mr Adventure he found posting letters into letter boxes rather boring.

So, to make it more interesting, he took his mountaineering gear to work with him and climbed the wall of each house and posted the letters down the chimney.

This certainly made delivering letters more interesting, however it also meant everybody's letters were late and covered in soot.

So he was told not to come back to work at the post office.

The next job he got was as a plumber.

And of course Mr Adventure found fitting pipes and repairing taps boring.

To make it more exciting Mr Adventure took his canoe to work when he went to fix a leak.

This definitely made plumbing more exciting, but it also made people's houses wetter.

Much, much wetter.

And so he was sacked from his plumbing job.

And it turned out that wearing skis to his building job was also not a very good idea.

Things were not going well.

Mr Adventure had not saved a penny.

He looked longingly at the map on his wall.

How he wished he could go on a proper adventure.

And then Mr Adventure got a new job.

A job as a firefighter.

A firefighter called to emergencies.

Emergencies like climbing a very tall tree to save a cat.

This was not boring.

The next day he had to break down a door with an axe.

This was definitely not boring.

And the next day he had to put out a fire in a burning house.

Mr Adventure had found a job that he liked.

A job that suited him down to the ground and right up to the top of the ladder.

In no time at all Mr Adventure had saved enough money to go on holiday.

Enough money to go to the wildest, remotest, most dangerous place you could think of in the whole wide world.

So where did Mr Adventure go?

Why, he stayed at home!

Being a fireman was a much greater adventure.